Dino-Saw

About the author/illustrator.

Jacqueline Ball lives in Plymouth with her family.
She co-founded the magical and award wining Stiltskin Arts
and the Soapbox Children's Theatre with her husband Iain.
The theatre is a place where children's imaginations
are ignited, using theatre, arts and storytelling,
all within the beautiful grounds of Devonport Park, Plymouth.

For my brilliant boys Iain, Zaq and Quinn.

Published by Stiltskin Arts
Plymouth, England

Registered publishing address
60 Elm Road, Plymouth, PL4 7BB

www.stiltskin.org.uk

A long,
long,
long, long, long,
long, long, looong,
time ago, a
CRACK!
rang out across the
valley of the Dinosaurs...

Baby-Dino began to explore...

Baby-Dino has met Danny Diplodocus.
Danny Diplodocus likes to play football.

Danny and Baby-Dino
play football
together.

Danny Diplodocus is hungry.
He stops playing to eat.
Plants are his favourite food.
Danny is always hungry.

Baby-Dino copies Danny Diplodocus
and also eats the plants.
Oh dear! Baby-Dino thinks that plants
taste disgusting. YUK!

But Danny Diplodocus looks TASTY.

Danny Diplodocus looks like a
giant green sausage.

Then Baby-Dino realises it is very bad table manners to eat your friends.

Baby-Dino and
Danny Diplodocus are friends.

Daddy Diplodocus
has come to take
Danny Diplodocus home.
Baby-Dino is all alone.
Can you roar to help him call
for his Mummy? ROOOAAARRRR!

Leaf
flies down from
the trees. Leaf and Baby-Dino are friends.

Baby-Dino climbs on board Leaf's back.
They are going on an adventure together.
Can you do a big blow to help
them on their way?
1,2,3, blow really hard.

Up and up and up they go.

Off they fly over the tops
of the trees and far away.

Over the Valley of the
Dinosaurs they went.

The Dinosaurs below
roared their awesome
roar...can you help them?
1,2,3 ROOOAAARRR!

On and on and on they flew.

Around and around and around.

Until they came to the sea...

Baby-Dino and Leaf
land on top of the sea.
Beneath the waves
are Jellyfish and
Ammonites.

A mummy and baby Plesiosaurus swim past playing in the bubbles.

Baby-Dino and leaf are ready to take off again.

Can you help them by blowing hard? WOW! Up and up and up they go, around and around and around...

Until they fly over a desert full of grey dust and past the VOLCANO!

Baby-Dino and Leaf land near the volcano.

The ground is shaking and rumbling.

Suddenly the volcano erupts with a BANG!

Oh No! Talula Triceratops is trapped on a rock floating on top of the lava.

Wow! Look, Daphne the diving Pterodactyl has come to the rescue.

Talula is a flying Triceratops; she is a Flyceratops. Bravo Daphne, Talula is safe.

Baby-Dino and Leaf fly home.

Leaf and Baby-Dino say goodbye.

Mummy T-Rex heard you ROAR earlier for Baby-Dino! She has brought him a bone.

YUM, YUM!

Printed in Poland
by Amazon Fulfillment
Poland Sp. z o.o., Wrocław